Perea

...ERTY OF CHAPTER I ECIA
... COUNTY SCHOOL DISTRICT
...LARAMIE, WYOMING

'85

Case of the
GREAT TRAIN ROBBERY

Written by Rae Bains
Illustrated by Paul Harvey

Troll Associates

Library of Congress Cataloging in Publication Data

Bains, Rae.
    Case of the great train robbery.

    (A Troll easy-to-read mystery)
    Summary: Mark and his pet skunk, Sheldon, outwit
a pair of train robbers.
    [1. Mystery and detective stories. 2. Skunks—
Fiction] I. Harvey, Paul, 1926-   ill. II. Ti-
tle.   III. Series: Troll easy-to-read mystery.
PZ7.B157Cas   [Fic]   81-7525
ISBN 0-89375-588-5 (lib. bdg.)   AACR2
ISBN 0-89375-589-3 (pbk.)

Copyright © 1982 by Troll Associates, Mahwah, New Jersey.
All rights reserved. No part of this book may be used or
reproduced in any manner whatsoever without written permission
from the publisher.
Printed in the United States of America.

10   9   8   7   6   5   4   3   2

Case of *the*
GREAT TRAIN
ROBBERY

WASHINGTON SCHOOL

Mark sat on the front steps. He watched the moving men work. They took lamps and chairs into the house. They carried in Mark's bed and his bike.

"I hope the kids are nice around here," Mark thought. "I hope I make friends soon."

Mark saw two boys. They were walking down the street. They were passing a basketball back and forth.

The boys stopped in front of the house. They looked at the moving men.

Then they looked at Mark.

Mark waved. "Hi," he said.

"Yuk! Let's get out of here," yelled one of the boys.

And they both ran away.

Mark watched the boys go. He knew why they ran away.

Mark looked down at the small, furry animal sitting next to him. It cuddled close to Mark. The boy patted his pet skunk on the head.

"Don't worry, Sheldon. I still love you," Mark said.

Mark took a small, red ball from his pocket. He threw it on the grass.

Sheldon bounced down the steps. He got the ball and ran back to Mark. He wagged his fluffy, striped tail.

"You're the best pet!" Mark said.

Sheldon licked Mark's hand.

Mark and his skunk were good friends. Sheldon liked to sleep on Mark's bed. They watched television together. Their favorite shows were Western movies, with cowboys and horses and train robberies.

Sheldon knew a lot of tricks, too. He could roll over. He could shake hands. And he could dancc on his back legs. He was a very smart skunk.

He was also a super watch-skunk.
When Mark said, "Stay!" Sheldon would
sit down and not move, until Mark said,
"Come here, Sheldon!"

Sheldon knew how to scare bullies
away. They never picked on Mark.
Sheldon just turned around and lifted his
tail. That made them run away fast!

Mark and Sheldon got up from the steps of their new house and walked down the street. They went around the corner. There was a playground. It was empty.

They walked some more. Soon they came to a stream near some woods. By jumping from stone to stone, they crossed the stream. Close by was a railroad track.

"Whoo-whooo!"

A train was coming. Mark and Sheldon sat down.

"Seven, eight, nine, ten," Mark said. "Look at the train, Sheldon. It has ten cars."

Sheldon yawned and stretched. Then he tugged at Mark's leg. He wanted to go home.

Suddenly, the train screeched to a
stop. A man climbed down from the front
of the train. He was wearing a mask. He
had a gun.

Mark grabbed Sheldon and hid behind
a tree.

"Harry!" the man shouted. "Did you get the money?"

Another masked man jumped off the back of the train. He had a sack in his hands. "Got it, Butch," he said. "Right here."

The two robbers ran into the woods.

"Gee, Sheldon. A real train robbery. Just like in the movies," said Mark.

The skunk bounced up and down. He was excited.

"We'll follow them. Come on," Mark whispered.

Mark and Sheldon ran after the robbers.

Mark could not see them. But he could hear them. He and Sheldon followed the sounds deeper into the woods.

Then the sounds stopped. There was no cracking of branches. No heavy footsteps. No talking.

"Okay, Sheldon," Mark said. "Now *you* find the trail."

The skunk sniffed the air. He sniffed the trees, the bushes, and the rocks.

Sheldon's eyes gleamed. He trotted off, with Mark right behind him.

They walked on and on. It was hot. They were tired. But they did not stop.

After a while they heard voices again. They tiptoed very quietly.

Then they saw a cave. It was almost hidden by the trees.

"You found it, Sheldon! The hide-out!"

"Wait here," Mark said. "I'm going closer."

He tried to move silently, like a spy in the movies. Then—"Oof!" Mark tripped on a rock. He fell hard.

"Who's there?" a gruff voice called.

Butch and Harry rushed out of the cave.

They saw Mark on the ground.

The robbers grabbed Mark.

"The kid followed us," Butch said.

"Yeah, we can't let him go," Harry said.

Mark was shaking.

"Anybody with you?" Butch growled.

"N-n-no," Mark managed to say. "I'm all a-l-l-lone. There is nobody here to save me." He hoped Sheldon was listening.

"You can bet nobody will save you," Harry said.

The robbers laughed.

They took Mark into a cave. Butch tied his hands and feet with rope. They sat him on a log.

The robbers sat in front of a fire. They ate, and talked.

"What do we do next?" Harry asked.

"We leave the money here. Then we get the car and come back later," Butch said.

"What about the kid?" Harry asked.

"After the money's in the car, we'll let him go, and make our getaway," Butch said.

"Yeah. We'll be far away before he can get to the cops," Harry said.

The robbers finished their lunch.

"See 'ya, kid," Harry said.

"Watch the money till we get back," said Butch. He laughed. They left the cave.

Mark was scared. He was hungry and lonely.

"I hope the robbers don't catch Sheldon," he said out loud.

Mark tried to untie the ropes. But they were too tight. He rubbed the ropes against the log. They would not tear.

Mark wished he was home. He began to cry.

Pit-pat. Pit-pat. Pit-pat. Pit-pat.

Mark stopped crying. He grinned.

"Sheldon!" he shouted. "You came to save me. You're a true friend!"

Mark held out his tied hands.

The skunk began to chew the ropes. He chewed and chewed until they came apart. Mark's hands were free.

"Good work, Sheldon," Mark said. And he took the rope off his feet.

Mark walked around the cave. He looked in the sack. It was filled with money.

Then he saw a cardboard box. He opened it.

"Guess what I found, Sheldon? Food!" he said.

The box had cheese and crackers in it. Mark shared the food with his pet. Then Sheldon curled up for a nap. He was a tired little skunk.

Mark rested his head on his hands and thought very hard. Soon he had a plan.

"I will go to the police," he thought. "I will tell them about the robbers. Sheldon can stay here to guard the money."

"Wake up, Sheldon," Mark said.

Sheldon opened his eyes. He stood up.

Mark pointed to the money sack and said, "Come here, Sheldon. You have a big job to do."

The skunk walked right by Mark. He went to the sack and jumped on it.

Mark clapped his hands. "You're one smart skunk!" he said. "Now stay there till I get back."

Sheldon sat down on the sack. He watched Mark go out of the cave.

Mark ran through the woods. He passed the railroad tracks and crossed the stream. Soon he came to town.

Mark ran on. At last he saw a police officer.

"Officer, officer!" he cried. "I want to report a crime!"

Mark told the police officer about the
robbery. He told about the cave in the
woods, and Sheldon guarding the money.

"Let's tell all this to the chief," the
officer said.

"Quick! Before the robbers get back to the cave and Sheldon," Mark said.

They hurried off to the police station.

Mark told everything to the chief of police. The chief told the mayor.

"Let's get rolling!" said the chief.

Ten police officers jumped into their cars.

"You must show us the way," the mayor told Mark. "You'll ride with me."

Mark and the mayor and the chief got into a big car.

The cars raced down the road. They came to the railroad track.

Mark pointed at the woods. "The cave is in there," he said.

"Everybody out," the chief said. "From here on, we walk." The ten officers got out of their cars. They drew their guns.

"Follow Mark," the chief said.

They ran into the woods. Mark led the
way. Deeper and deeper they went.

Suddenly, the mayor stopped. "*Phew!
What is that smell?*" he asked.

"That's Sheldon," said Mark.
"Something must have happened."

"Let's hurry," said the chief. His voice
sounded funny. He was holding his nose.
So was the mayor. So were the ten police
officers.

The smell led them right to the cave.

"Sheldon! Sheldon! Are you all
right?" Mark called.

He dashed into the cave. The officers
and the chief and the mayor were right
behind him.

There was Sheldon. Sitting on top of
the money sack.

"Look. The money is safe," said the
chief.

"What does Sheldon have in his mouth?" the mayor asked.

Mark walked up to Sheldon. "It's a piece of cloth," he said.

The cloth was blue, with green stripes.

"I know what the cloth is from," Mark said. "Butch's pants!"

The mayor patted Sheldon on the head. "You are a real watch-skunk," he said.

"We have the money. Now we must get the robbers," said the chief.

The mayor looked worried. "That will be hard to do. These woods are big. And it will be dark soon."

Mark smiled. "Sheldon made it easy for us. He sprayed his smell on them."

Everybody left the cave. They sniffed the air. They followed the smell.

The smell got stronger. And stronger.

And the hunt was soon over. There were the robbers, sitting in the middle of the stream in their underwear.

"Going swimming, boys?" asked the chief.

Everybody giggled — except the robbers.

"It's not funny," Butch shouted.

"A wild skunk attacked us," Harry groaned.

"Don't worry," said the mayor. "You'll get a bath and a new suit—in jail."

The police handcuffed the robbers
and took them away.

"You deserve a medal for this, young
man," said the chief.

"Not me," said Mark. "Sheldon did it all."

"Both of you will get medals. Tomorrow. At City Hall," said the mayor.

The next day Mark and Sheldon went to City Hall. There were TV cameras and people from the newspaper.

The mayor told everybody how brave
Mark was. And the chief of police praised
Sheldon's bravery. The mayor gave big
gold medals to Mark and Sheldon.
Everyone clapped and cheered.

When Mark got home there were lots of kids waiting to see him. They wanted to meet the hero. They wanted to hear about the robbery and the cave. And everything.

They shook Mark's hand. They petted Sheldon.

Mark was glad to tell his new friends the whole story.

Sheldon just yawned, and went to sleep.

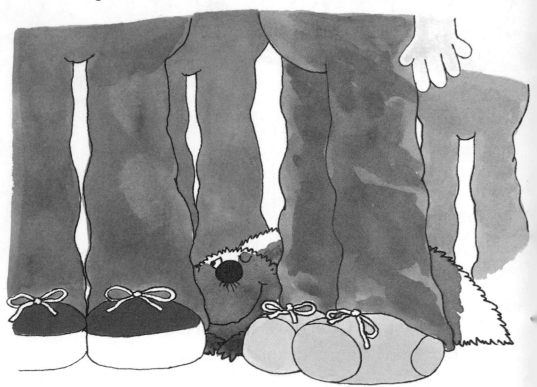